NO PROBLEM, DAVY

Davy remembered what his dad had said. He must not untie the lead from the post. But what difference was it going to make? He would just let Patch have a little run, then tie him up again. Dogs needed to run around, didn't they? He reached out and unclipped the lead. No problem...

Before Davy could stop him, Patch dashed away down the road.

Davy stared after him in horror.

For a special young lady
Abigail Christen Metcalfe

NO PROBLEM, DAVY

Peggy Burns

Illustrations by Helen Herbert

A LION PAPERBACK
Oxford · Batavia · Sydney

Text copyright © 1991 Peggy Burns
Illustrations copyright © 1991 Helen Herbert

Published by
Lion Publishing plc
Sandy Lane West, Oxford, England
ISBN 0 7459 2076 4
Albatross Books Pty Ltd
PO Box 320, Sutherland, NSW 2232, Australia
ISBN 0 7324 0489 4

First edition 1991
All rights reserved

British Library Cataloguing in Publication Data
Burns, Peggy
    No problem, Davy.
    I. Title
    823[J]
    ISBN 0 7459 2076 4

Printed and bound in Great Britain by
Cox and Wyman Ltd, Reading

CONTENTS

1

The Very Special Present

Davy rode his bike slowly up and down the pavement in front of his house. He watched as a big red van with writing on the side pulled up outside the empty house next door. A blue Ford Sierra drove up and stopped in the driveway.

A boy got out of the car. He stared at Davy. Davy stared back.

'My name's Davy,' said Davy. 'What's yours?'

'Oliver,' said the boy. 'We're coming to live in this house.'

Davy smiled. The only other boy who lived nearby was Gary Smith, and he was ten. It would be great having a next-door friend. 'Do you want to play?' he asked Oliver.

'Wait till they take my bike out of the van, then I will,' said Oliver. He looked at Davy's bike. 'It's newer than yours. I can do wheelies on it.'

The boys watched two men carry beds and tables and boxes into the house. It took them a long time to get to Oliver's bike, because it was right at the back of the van. At last they lifted it out.

Oliver was taller than Davy, so his bike was bigger than Davy's. It was a brilliant red and yellow stunt bike, with a big silver horn fixed to the handlebars. Oliver rode off down the street. He made the bike rear up on one wheel just like Gary Smith did. Then he twirled round and round on it.

Davy watched him. He couldn't do wheelies on his bike. It wasn't the right kind—he always fell off when he tried. 'Let me have a go on your bike,' he asked Oliver.

'No way,' said Oliver. 'I'm not allowed to let anyone else ride it. It cost a lot of money.'

Davy watched Oliver doing stunts for a long time. Then they went to Davy's house for a snack.

Davy's mum smiled at Oliver. She was pleased that Davy had a new friend. She made them both an orange drink and put some chocolate biscuits on a plate. Oliver tasted his drink—and pulled a face.

'What's wrong with it?' asked Davy.

'My mum only buys fresh orange juice,' Oliver said. 'I don't like this kind.'

Davy's mum was surprised. 'I'm sorry you don't like it,' she said. 'I haven't got any fresh orange juice. Would you like a biscuit instead?'

Oliver took a biscuit and did not say 'Thank you'.

'Fresh orange juice!' said Davy as they went back outside. 'What's wrong with our kind of orange?'

'My mum says it has too much sugar in it, and it makes your teeth go rotten.'

'It doesn't.'

'Yes, it does. And it makes you fat, too.'

'It does not. I'm not fat!'

'You're not thin, either. But your mother's fat . . . It's with drinking orange squash, I bet.'

Davy almost told Oliver that Mum had a baby in her tummy—then decided not to say anything. Why should Oliver know all his secrets? 'Well, she's better than your mother, anyway.'

'She is not.'

'She's a million times better.'

'You've never seen my mother. Mine's a billion times better than yours. And she's not fat. She buys better biscuits, as well.' Oliver got on his bike and rode away. 'She's a million, trillion times better than yours,' he shouted over his shoulder.

'Oh, shut up,' Davy muttered. Some friend he'd turned out to be.

But that was just the beginning.

Oliver was in the same class as Davy. He went to Davy's birthday party with some other boys from school. The party was at Davy's house. Davy's mum baked special chocolate buns with green, mint-flavoured icing on top. She made a red jelly shaped like a spaceship, and there were tons of ice cream.

'I'm having my birthday party at the village hall,' Oliver announced. 'And I'm having a Punch and Judy show.'

He looked through Davy's presents and sniffed scornfully at the green jumper with the red train on it that Davy's grandma had knitted.

'My jumper came from Togs,' he told Davy. Togs was the posh clothes shop in the High Street that Davy's mum never went to. Suddenly, Grandma West's knitting didn't seem so special.

'Oh—you got one of those,' said Oliver, opening Davy's Space Turbo game box. That was his very best present from Mum and Dad.

'I had one last year,' Oliver went on. 'I soon got tired of it. What's this? Oh—a Battleship game. Mine's electronic. It lights up. I'm getting a go-kart for my birthday.'

Davy sighed. Was there anything he had that

Oliver didn't already have that was bigger, better and more exciting?

When the party was over, Davy's mum flopped on to the sofa. She looked tired, Davy noticed. He sat down next to her and she put her arm around him and cuddled him close. He didn't always like it when she did that, but tonight it felt good. Mum was warm and soft and she smelled of baking and hair shampoo. And she was the best mum in the world.

'Oliver's Battleship Game is electronic,' he told her, wriggling around to look up into her face.

'Oh, is it?' she said.

'And Oliver's jumper came from Togs. It's better than mine.'

Mum ruffled his hair. 'Things that cost a lot aren't always better,' she said wisely. 'Your jumper has got special stitches in it.'

Davy frowned. 'What kind of special stitches?'

'Love stitches,' she said, smiling, her eyes crinkling at the corners. Davy loved the way her eyes crinkled.

She went on. 'Oliver's jumper was only bought from a shop. But your jumper is very special, because Grandma West knitted love into every single stitch, just for you!'

Davy smiled, thinking about Grandma West sitting in her chair and knitting away, clickety-click. Knitting love into the jumper with her funny, bent fingers as she went along. The jumper was great—and so was Grandma.

He put his arms around his mum's waist and hid his face in her fat tummy.

'It's good about the jumper,' he told her. 'But I wish I had something that was all mine ... Something Oliver hasn't got.'

He sighed deeply. Mum always said that when you were feeling down, God knew all about it. Suddenly he said, 'Do you think it would be all right if I asked God for something very special? Even more special than a jumper with love stitches?'

He looked up at his mum. Her eyes were sparkling and she was smiling and smiling as if she knew a special secret.

'I'm sure he wouldn't mind if you asked him that,' Mum told him. 'But just remember—it's people, not things, that matter. I think Oliver boasts all the time because he's trying to make people like him. What he needs is a friend.'

That night when Dad came to do goodnight

prayers with him, Davy asked God about some-thing special. And he talked to him about Oliver, too. 'I'm so tired of him showing off all the time!' he said. 'But if he needs a friend, then I'll try ...'

When he woke up in the morning, Auntie Beth was in the kitchen instead of Mum, making break-fast. Why was she there? Auntie Beth was nice, but he wanted Mum; she always cooked his egg a special way.

'Where's my mum?' he asked Auntie Beth.

She bent down and put her arm around his shoulders. 'Remember the new baby your mum and dad told you about? The baby started to come during the night and Mum had to go away to hospital, so I came across to look after you.'

'When's she coming back?' Davy's voice was very small.

'Soon. A lot depends on how quickly that baby comes. She wanted to tell you about it herself, but you were fast asleep and she didn't want to wake you. She told me to tell you she loves you a lot and she'll come back just as soon as she can.'

Davy understood. Babies had to be born. But it wasn't the same without Mum. Auntie Beth boiled his egg longer than Mum did, and it tasted different. And his toast was pale instead of being crunchy round the edges.

Davy was miserable all morning at school. Was his mum really all right? When would she come back? At dinner time Auntie Beth met him at the school gate and took him home for lunch.

'There's a surprise waiting for you,' she told him as they walked up the garden path.

'Mum's come back!' Davy cried eagerly.

'Not yet. But someone else is here. Run in and see who it is.'

Davy ran into the house. His dad was there. In the middle of the day.

'Why aren't you at work?' Davy asked him. 'When will Mum come back?'

His dad grabbed him and swung him up to the ceiling, just like he used to when Davy was little. Dad was excited about something.

'Remember what you talked to God about last night?'

Davy nodded. How could he forget?

'He's answered your prayer already. Get ready for the very best present you've ever had!'

'The new baby's come!' Davy shouted.

Dad swung him up again.

'Right first time. You have a baby sister!' Dad said. 'She's called Amy. Amy is your special present!'

'How soon will she be able to play football?' asked Davy. Dad just chuckled.

'Your mum's in hospital, isn't she?' said Oliver that afternoon. 'I heard my mum talking to your auntie.'

Davy smiled to himself.

'She's coming home tomorrow,' he told Oliver. 'She's got a special present for me. I've got a brand-new baby sister!'

He waited for Oliver to speak.

But for once, Oliver had nothing at all to say.

2
Everything Used To Be Mine

Davy watched Dad painting the cot he'd slept in when he was a baby.

Up and down the brush went, leaving a coat of smooth, shiny white where it had been blue before. The blue rabbits on the back of the cot slowly turned white. Soon there were no rabbits left at all. Everything was white. At last, Dad stood back and admired his handiwork.

'There!' he said proudly, wiping his painty hands on a cloth. 'It's finished. Doesn't that look smart, Davy?'

'Are you going to put some more rabbits on it?' Davy asked him.

'Kittens this time,' Dad said, and winked at him. He put the lid back on his can of paint, picked it up and went off to put it away in the shed.

Davy looked at the cot.

He hadn't slept in it for a long time, of course. He had a big bed now. But he remembered how much he had loved those rabbits. Now they were gone. Kittens would be there instead. Kittens for the new baby.

His new baby sister was called Amy. Davy hadn't even seen Amy yet, but today he was going with Dad to the hospital to bring her and Mum home.

All the grown-ups were very excited about the new baby—even Grandma West, who often sounded cross when she wasn't cross at all, and who hardly ever got excited about anything. Grandma West had been busy for weeks and weeks knitting tiny coats and bonnets, counting stitches and muttering, 'Knit one, purl two, knit two together.' But she was never too busy knitting to talk to Davy.

'Come on, Davy—let's go!' Dad shouted up the stairs. He had combed his hair and washed the paint off his hands with some smelly stuff out of a bottle, and now he was putting on his jacket.

He helped Davy into his new jumper. The one Grandma West had knitted with the special stitches. 'We haven't got much time,' Dad said. 'The painting took longer than I thought. And we mustn't be late bringing Mum and Amy home, must we?'

Davy wasn't sure. 'Will Amy sleep in my cot tonight?' he asked.

Dad laughed. 'The paint will still be wet, son. But in any case, the cot is too big for her just now. New babies are very tiny. She'll sleep in the carrycot in our room until she gets bigger.'

Davy pushed his feet into his blue trainers. 'Did that used to be my carrycot, too?'

Dad nodded. 'It's good not to have to buy a new one,' he said. 'They're very expensive.'

Amy is taking everything that used to be mine, thought Davy. He wasn't sure he liked that.

His cot. His carrycot. Even his bedroom was going to be Amy's room. Davy's racing cars wallpaper was now covered up with puppies and kittens paper, and the newly-painted cot stood in a corner. Davy's bed and furniture had been put in the spare room, which was bigger. There was new wallpaper here, too, with spaceships on it.

'You're growing up,' Mum had said. 'You deserve a big new bedroom.'

Davy thought the spaceships were great—but still, he had liked his little bedroom. He felt a bit lost in the new one.

At the hospital Mum was waiting for them, wearing a big smile and looking just the same, only thinner. She hugged Davy tight and Davy squirmed because a nurse was watching. 'Look at your new sister,' Mum said.

The nurse, wearing a blue uniform, held Amy out for him to see.

'Isn't she beautiful?' said Davy's dad.

Davy didn't think so. Amy was pink and wrinkled and as bald as old Mr Parker across the street.

'She looks old!' Davy said, and was surprised when Mum and Dad laughed.

'Her hair will soon grow,' said the nurse, tying a little pink bonnet on to the baby's head. Davy remembered Grandma West knitting it.

Mum had a parcel in her hand. She gave it to Davy. 'Open it,' she said. 'It's a present from Amy.'

A present? Quickly, Davy tore off the wrapping. Inside was a cardboard box, and in the box was a shiny red dumper truck.

Davy looked again at his new sister. Of course, the truck was from Mum and Dad really—he knew Amy was too little to go to the shops. But still, it was a good truck.

'Thank you, Amy,' he said, but Amy was fast asleep and took no notice.

Grandma and Grandad West came around that

afternoon to see the new baby. They brought presents with them, a tiny pink dress and more knitted jackets for Amy.

Grandma West was very fat and had a wide, comfortable lap that was soft to sit on. Even now he was big, Davy liked to sit on her knee at bedtime and listen to stories. But today Grandma just ruffled his hair and held Amy on her knee instead. Mum's friend, Auntie Susan, visited them too, and brought a white stretchy suit for the new baby.

'Nobody brought me a present,' Davy told Dad when all the visitors had gone home and it was bedtime. 'All the presents were for Amy.'

'Amy brought you a present,' Dad reminded him.

Davy climbed slowly into bed and Dad sat down by his side, like he often did, to say prayers. Talking to God was very important, Dad said.

Tonight one of Dad's prayers was, 'Thank you, God, for giving Amy to us.'

Davy screwed his eyes tightly shut. He had a funny, heavy feeling in his tummy. He was wondering whether having a new sister was going to be as special as he'd thought.

He wouldn't exactly pray that God would take

Amy away again—but he did not feel excited any more.

Life, Davy soon found, was very different with a baby in the house. Amy went to sleep at funny times, and Davy often had to keep quiet when he didn't feel like it. And in between her long sleeps Amy made a very loud noise for such a tiny person.

Davy did enjoy taking her out in her pram, though. Summer gradually turned to autumn, and every day after school—when it wasn't raining—he and Mum would wheel Amy down the hill to the park. In the playground, Davy swung on the swings, climbed up the high slide, and rode on the rocking-horse that had a head like a dragon.

'When will Amy be big enough to ride on the rocking-horse?' asked Davy one windy day on the way to the park.

'In year or so, if I sit with her and hold her,' his mother said. The wind was strong, and she held on to her red woolly hat with one hand.

'Oh.' Davy ran on, losing interest. A year was too long even to think about. He stirred up the carpet of red and gold leaves around his feet, kicking them about. Some of them blew away in the wind. Others, wet and slimy, stuck fast to the pavement.

'Why do the leaves go brown and fall off the trees?' was his next question. He picked some up and threw them into the air. The wind caught them and whisked them away.

'Because winter is coming and the tree has finished with them for this year. Next spring it will grow new ones.'

At that moment, an extra hard gust of wind whipped Davy's hood off his head. Mum clutched again at her hat.

At the same time, the heel of her shoe skidded on the wet, slimy leaves. Her foot slid away beneath her and she fell backwards and down on to the pavement. As Mum fell, she let go of the pram.

'Davy!' she screamed.

Slowly at first, the pram rolled away from them, then it picked up speed. Davy's eyes widened in horror. At the bottom of the slope was the wide, busy main road.

Mum was struggling to her feet, but Davy was running, running ... pushing himself as fast as he could go, his heart hammering, his trainers pounding on the pavement.

Mum had called his name. Mum was depending on him. He slipped, got his balance, and ran on

again, down the hill after the pram.

'Please, God—save Amy!' He said the words over and over again inside his head.

He grabbed at the pram, missed it, then flung himself forward and grabbed again. This time his hand closed tightly around the handle and, his feet skidding on the ground, Davy jerked the runaway pram to a standstill.

Still trembling, he jammed on the pram's brake, then looked down at his little sister.

Amy hadn't enjoyed being shaken about. Her mouth opened—a pink, gummy cave—and she began to wail. It was a loud, cross noise. 'Oh, Amy!' Davy laughed. 'You don't need to cry now. You're quite safe!' And his gladness was the warm, happy feeling of love.

He bent over and kissed the angry red face, and was surprised when the wailing stopped. Amy gazed up at Davy with big dark eyes—and suddenly, the baby smiled. Davy smiled back. The two of them smiled and smiled at each other, then Davy carefully tucked a tiny waving arm under the covers.

Mum, looking very pale, ran up to them. Without a word she put both arms around Davy and held him very close.

'My grown-up, clever boy!' she said. And Davy felt proud.

He was growing up. And suddenly, he didn't mind having a baby sister any more.

3

Kalimera, Davy!

Davy was very excited. He was going on an aeroplane for the very first time. He was going on holiday with Mum and Dad and baby Amy to an island called Corfu.

'Corfu is hotter than England,' Dad told him. 'So we'll be able to swim in the sea and play on the beach and wear our shorts all the time. Won't that be great?'

Davy thought it would. He could hardly wait.

At last, Mum and Dad started packing suitcases. Mum found all the clothes and things they would need in Corfu and piled them up on the bed. Then Dad put them all neatly into two big cases. There were so many things that Davy thought Dad would never get the lids shut, but at last the cases stood in the hallway, closed and locked.

Dad drove them to the airport and parked the car. Then they all stood for a very long time in a queue until the cases and Amy's push-chair were taken away to be put on to the plane. After that, they went to look around the shops in the airport.

There were lots of interesting things to look at, but even so, Davy was glad when it was time to get on the plane. A very smiley lady looked at their tickets, told them where to sit, and ruffled Davy's hair.

Davy sat by the window, and Mum buckled a seat-belt around his middle. He looked out across the airport. There were lots of other planes standing around. As he watched, another one flew down, lower and lower, then landed.

Their own plane set off, quite slowly at first. Then they went faster and faster, and Davy held on tight to Mum's hand. Suddenly they were in the air, and the airport was below them. Houses and roads were spread out underneath like a toy village. Then there were only clouds below, looking solid enough to walk on. Davy let out a breath, and let go of Mum's hand.

It was all very exciting. After a while, the same smiley lady came around and gave everyone a plastic tray of dinner. Davy liked it, but he couldn't eat it all. He suddenly felt very tired. His head began to nod . . .

'Wake up, Davy. We're here.' Mum was shaking his shoulder. 'The plane is landing.'

What? Had he been asleep? Davy rubbed his eyes and sat up. He looked out of the window just in time to see green hills. Then he glimpsed small, square houses and big hotels. There was a gentle bump and the plane was down.

A coach took them to their hotel. A man with very black hair and twinkly eyes gave Dad the key to their room. He smiled down at Davy.

'Are you hungry?' the man asked. 'Your dinner is waiting for you.'

But Davy yawned a big pink yawn. 'I'm not hungry,' he told the man sleepily. All he wanted to do was go to bed.

And the next thing he knew, it was morning. Davy didn't remember getting into his pyjamas, but here he was wearing them, and lying in a strange bed.

'So you're awake at last!' Mum said, bending over him. 'Amy has been awake for ages, and she's had her breakfast. You'd better hurry up and get dressed if you want to eat—the waiter will be clearing the tables soon!'

In the dining-room, the same twinkly man brought them a plate piled high with bread rolls, and a basket of tiny jars of jam. Davy chose strawberry and spread it thickly on his bread and butter.

Then the man brought tea and coffee for Mum and Dad, and orange juice for Davy. 'My name is Spiro,' he told Davy. 'What's yours?'

'Davy,' said Davy.

'*Kalimera*, Davy,' said Spiro, and Davy stared at him.

'That's Greek, Davy,' said Dad. 'The people here speak a language of their own. It's called Greek.'

'So what does that mean? *Kal*—, *kal*— something?'

'*Kalimera*,' Spiro told him. 'That means "Good morning".'

Davy was very interested. You could say words in a different language that meant the same as English words. '*Kalimera*, Spiro,' he said, and Spiro laughed.

'You learn fast,' he said, tweaking Davy's ear.

After breakfast they walked down a long village street lined with shops, then down another short lane which led to the beach. Mum sat on a sun bed, took a bottle of sun cream out of her bag and rubbed it all over Amy and Davy. Then she tied a little white sun bonnet on Amy's head and rubbed cream over her own arms and legs. Davy ran off to splash about in the water, leaving Mum to sunbathe while Amy took a nap in her push-chair.

Davy had a wonderful time. He played ball with another boy who was on holiday too. He found a rock pool with crabs in it, and tiny fish swimming around. He watched Dad throw flat stones that skimmed across the sea, bouncing off the tops of the waves. Davy tried to do it too, but whenever he threw stones they fell into the sea with a plop.

After a late lunch, Dad went off on his own, looking very mysterious. He came back driving a car.

'Now we'll be able to look around the island properly,' he said.

Dad drove them into the town. Corfu town was very different from English towns. The streets were narrow and the houses were very tall. All the windows had shutters to keep out the hot sun.

In a narrow alley, an old, old lady passed them. She was dressed in a black headscarf and a long black dress that reached right to the ground. Davy thought she must be very hot. He was glad he was wearing his shorts.

The old lady smiled down at Davy. '*Yasu*,' she said.

'*Kalimera*,' replied Davy, and the old lady laughed and patted his shoulder.

'What does "*Yasu*" mean?' Davy asked his Dad.

'I think it means "Hello",' Dad said.

Davy smiled to himself. Now he knew two Greek words, '*Yasu, kalimera. Yasu, kalimera*'. Hello, good morning. Only it wasn't morning any more. He wondered what the Greek word for 'Good afternoon' was.

They walked along a street of shops, looking into all the windows. The signs above the shops were written in strange writing that even Dad couldn't read. Mum bought a straw hat to keep the sun off her head, and a blue cap for Davy.

At the end of the street was a wide, green square. Some men were playing cricket there. They walked around the cricket pitch and through a garden full of flowers. Then Davy stopped and stared.

There, in front of him, all lined up like taxis in a rank, was a row of horses and carriages, all gaily decorated with brightly coloured ribbons and plumes. Some of the horses were wearing straw hats to keep their heads cool. 'Oh!' cried Davy, running forward. He'd never seen a horse wearing a hat before. 'Can we ride in one, Dad? Please?'

Dad laughed. 'If you like.'

A man with white hair and a shiny gold tooth at the front of his mouth took the money Dad gave him, and they all climbed into the carriage.

The horse went a lot slower than a car, but Davy decided that he liked this way much better. When you weren't going so fast, you could see much more. And there was an awful lot to see.

They drove past colourful gardens and open-air cafés with bright yellow chairs arranged in the cool shade of the trees. They drove down a long hill alongside the bluest sea Davy had ever seen. They drove along a wide avenue of tall houses and shops, then along a busy street full of cars and bikes and people on holiday wearing shorts and sun hats. Here and there were stalls and barrows piled high with apples, peaches, melons, bananas, oranges and lemons. Davy thought he'd like to buy a peach.

Lots of little side-streets branched away uphill. At the bottom of one of the streets a car was moving to and fro, trying to turn around in the narrow space. On the street corner stood one of the barrows of delicious fruit. The lady who was looking after the barrow smiled up at Davy as the carriage drew near.

'*Yasu!*' she called out to him.

Davy opened his mouth to say '*Kalimera!*'—but before he could say the word, the back bumper of the reversing car went *Crump!* straight into the side of the fruit barrow. The lady squealed and jumped out of the way just in time—before the barrow tipped up and fell over with a crash.

Apples and lemons, oranges and melons tipped over and spilled across the pavement, then rolled into the road right into the path of the horse and carriage.

Their horse was not used to stepping on a stream of bumping, bouncing oranges and lemons.

It let out a neigh of fright, then took off down the road as fast as it could go. People scattered as the horse and carriage raced towards them, jolting and bumping. The driver yelled at the horse in a stream of fast Greek that Davy couldn't understand. Mum squealed as her brand new hat bounced off her head and whipped away into the watching crowd of people. The horse's own straw hat slipped sideways and tipped over one eye. The horse raced on.

Davy leant forward, enjoying himself.

'Gee up!' he shouted to the horse. 'Get along there!'

The galloping horse turned the corner at the end of the road. The carriage swayed wildly. 'Giddy up!' Davy shouted again, and the horse ran on.

But it was a very long time since the horse had run so fast, and in the hot sun, too. It suddenly felt very tired. It slowed to a trot, then to a walk. The driver pulled on the reins. The horse stopped, blowing heavily.

Davy was very disappointed.

The driver sighed, then turned around in his seat and spoke to Davy's dad. 'I am sorry you had such a rough ride,' he said. 'I will take you around again if you like.'

'Oh, yes please!' cried Davy, eagerly.

'Er ... no thank you,' said Dad.

'It's very kind of you, but I think we'll get out here,' Mum said rather shakily.

Davy jumped out of the carriage with Mum and Dad. But he thought it was a pity they weren't going to go around again.

He liked Corfu, he decided. It was a very exciting place. He liked paddling in the warm, blue sea, and making new friends. He liked looking for crabs and fish in the pools among the rocks. He liked learning new words in the language that was written in squiggles.

But the very best thing about Corfu, Davy thought, was that brilliant ride in a rattling, bouncing carriage behind a galloping black horse wearing pink ribbons and a straw sun hat.

4
No Problem

Davy had been saving up for his holiday for a very long time. Every week, instead of buying sweets, he had put his pocket money into his money-box so that he would have lots to spend in Corfu.

'You won't be able to spend English money in Corfu,' Dad had told him. 'In Corfu they have Greek money.' And when they had arrived at their hotel he had asked a man to exchange Davy's English money for some Greek money.

'No problem!' the man had said.

Davy spread his money out on his bed and looked at it. Greek money was different from English money. There were two brown bank notes and a lot of coins that Dad said were called drachmas. Davy felt very rich.

'This will buy millions of ice creams!' he said, building all the coins into a tall pile in the middle of his bed.

Mum looked up at him. She was tying Amy's

sun bonnet strings. 'You should be careful how you spend it,' she told him. 'Don't waste your money.'

'Then what shall I buy with it?'

Mum thought for a minute, then said, 'Why not keep most of it until you see something really special that you can take back home with you? Something that will always remind you of your holiday in Corfu.' Davy thought that was a good idea. He wouldn't be able to take ice cream home with him. He put his money away again.

They all went outside to the hotel swimming-pool. It was a deep blue colour. Next to it there was grass to play on, and there were flower-beds, and small tables where people could sit under yellow-striped umbrellas sipping glasses of lemonade. And surprisingly, behind a fence was a hen-run, with lots of hens pecking and scratching and making a quiet burbling sound.

Mum sat on the edge of the pool and held Amy where she could kick and splash her legs in the water. Dad dived into the deep end of the pool and swam down the length of it. 'Come on in,' he shouted to Davy. 'It's great!'

Davy couldn't swim yet, though he was learning. He carefully lowered himself into the water at the shallow end of the pool. The sun was hot, but the water felt cold on Davy's warm skin. 'It's freezing!' he shouted. The water came up to his middle.

Mum threw a big green and yellow ball into the water, and Dad threw it to Davy. It landed with a slap in front of him, spraying cold water over him. He gasped as the cold drops ran down his chest, and Dad laughed.

'You wait!' Davy shouted. 'I'll get you for that!'

He reached for the ball and hurled it at Dad as hard as he could. It hit Dad in the chest and bounced back into the water.

'Oof!' Dad spluttered. 'Right in the middle— Ow! Two can play at that game!'

The ball came at Davy, swift and low. Davy jumped out of the way—but he lost his footing, slid sideways and went down full length into the water. He swallowed what felt like a gallon of pool water, and came up coughing and choking.

'Are you all right?' Dad shouted, but Davy didn't answer. Still coughing, he picked up the ball and lobbed it back at Dad without stopping to aim properly.

The ball soared upwards, then fell to the ground—but it landed behind the fence, among the hens. With a babble of frantic clucking, the hens scattered in every direction.

'Oh, no!' groaned Davy. 'What now?'

'You could ask Spiro to get the ball back for you,' said Mum.

Davy liked Spiro. He found him clearing tables in the dining-room. *'Kalimera*, Spiro,' Davy said, trying out the Greek he had learnt.

'Yasu, Davy-mou,' cried Spiro. 'What can I do for you?'

Davy told him about the ball. 'Please will you get it back for me?' he asked.

Spiro laughed his great laugh. 'No problem!' he said.

He went outside with Davy. Then he walked down the road a little way until he came to the gate of the hen-run. He went inside, picked up the ball, then shut the gate again. He took the ball back to Davy.

'Thank you very much,' said Davy.

'We're sorry we troubled you,' Dad told him.

'No problem!' Spiro chuckled, waving a brown hand at them. 'No problem!' At lunchtime they sat under the blue-striped canopy in front of the hotel and ate salad with sharp white cheese and crispy bread rolls and butter.

The pudding was fruit salad. Spiro put a dish in

front of Davy. '*Fruto salata*,' he said.

Davy looked at it. 'We had *fruto salata* yester-day,' he said. 'Please could I have some ice cream instead?'

'Davy!' Mum said. 'Mind your manners.'

But Spiro laughed. 'You like ice cream—ice cream you shall have!' he said. 'No problem!'

After lunch, they went to the beach. The sun was hot and Davy wore his blue cap and a pair of sunglasses. He paddled in the sea and watched people sailing around the bay in little red boats that had pedals like bicycles. Dad said they were called pedalos.

'Can we ride in a pedalo, Dad?' said Davy. 'Please?'

So Dad paid some money to a lady who smiled broadly at Davy. 'Have a good time,' she said.

Davy and Dad sat in the front seats, where the pedals were. Mum said she would rather sunbathe, so she sat at the back with Amy.

Pedalling a boat was fun, Davy thought. Hard work, but fun. He looked over the side into the clear blue-green water. It was very shallow, and he could see small groups of tiny fish swimming around among the clumps of seaweed. Then a bigger fish swam by. Davy leant over to see it

better—and plop, his sunglasses slid off his nose
and straight down into the sea.

'My glasses!' shouted Davy.

Dad stopped pedalling and the boat stopped

moving. Dad swung his legs over the side and jumped down into the water. It was only as deep as his knees. He felt around under the water among the rocks and the seaweed until, after a few minutes, his fingers felt the sunglasses.

'Got them!' he said.

But when he brought them up out of the water, there was only one dark lens in them. Davy put them on straight away, and Mum laughed.

'You look funny with one black eye and one ordinary one,' she said. So Davy decided to keep them on. He liked looking funny.

They pedalled around some more, then it was time to take the boat back. Davy jumped out and tried to pull the pedalo up on to the beach. It was very heavy.

'I'll do it,' Dad said, taking Amy from Mum as she jumped out of the boat.

But the pedalo lady was already pulling on the front of the boat. 'Leave it to me,' she said. 'No problem!'

Everything here is 'no problem' Davy thought, smiling to himself.

But Davy had a problem. He still didn't know what to spend his money on—and the holiday was nearly over.

Every day he gazed into every shop window they passed to see if there was anything really special that he could buy to take back to England with him. He saw lots of nice things: toy cars, sailing boats, games, balls. But nothing seemed special enough.

They made one last trip into the town. 'You might see something here that you want to buy,' said his mum.

They stopped outside a large gift shop that seemed to sell everything. Davy gazed at the racks of goods that stood along the pavement. What should he buy? There were so many things to choose from.

'What about a nice leather belt?' Mum suggested. 'That would look smart with your best trousers.'

But Davy wrinkled his nose. Belts were boring.

Davy looked at a row of beakers that had colourful pictures of Greek people dancing. He picked one up. It played a little tune.

'A mug is a good idea,' Mum said. 'You could drink your bedtime cocoa out of it and listen to the song at the same time.'

'Hmm. Maybe.' Davy put the mug down again and looked around some more.

'What about a clock for your bedroom wall?' said Dad. The clocks were nice; they had scenes of Corfu painted on them. But Davy already had a Mickey Mouse clock.

He sighed. 'I'm never going to find anything!' he said glumly as they walked on down the street. Wouldn't it be awful if he had to take all his money back home again. But just at that moment, he looked around and saw the very thing.

It was hanging up outside a clothes shop—the last kind of shop Davy would ever think of looking into, as clothes were boring.

'That's it!' he shouted, pointing, and Mum and Dad turned around and stared.

There, hanging together with a lot of shorts and shirts and swimming costumes, was a blue T-shirt. But Davy had seen straight away that this was no ordinary shirt. This particular T-shirt was very special, because across the front, in big black letters, it said *NO PROBLEM*.

'*NO PROBLEM*. That's just the thing to remind me of Corfu!' said Davy.

Mum held the shirt up in front of him. It was exactly the right size. He paid for the shirt. Then straight away he took off the top he was wearing and put on the new one.

When they got back to the hotel and Spiro saw it, he slapped Davy on the back and laughed his deep, hearty laugh. 'No problem!' he chuckled, looking at the shirt. 'You will have no problem remembering me, Davy-mou!'

'I'll always remember you, Spiro,' Davy told him.

Then there was only one morning left. They were going home. Mum and Dad packed most of their clothes back into the cases again. She wanted to pack the NO PROBLEM T-shirt, but Davy wanted to wear it.

After breakfast Davy and Dad went outside to have one last swim in the pool. Davy could swim three strokes now before he had to put his foot on the bottom. That morning, he swam four strokes. Dad was proud of him. 'You'll be swimming like a fish in no time,' he said.

Just then, Mum came outside and called them to lunch. 'We must hurry,' she said. 'There isn't much time. The coach is taking us to the airport at one, and it's twelve o'clock already.'

They had a quick lunch of Greek cheese pies and salad, then Dad carried the cases down to the hotel entrance. The coach pulled up outside, and Spiro helped Dad to load their cases into the big boot.

'Be good,' he told Davy. 'Eat plenty of *fruto salata!*'

And then they were off. As the coach drew away, Spiro waved madly. Davy waved back through the window.

'Come and sit down, Davy,' said his mum when they couldn't see Spiro any more.

'No problem!' Davy said . . . then quickly added, 'Oh, no!'

'What's the matter?'

'My shirt! I left it by the side of the pool!'

Davy wanted to ask the driver to go back to the hotel, but Dad said they couldn't do that because they had a plane to catch. Davy hadn't cried for a long time, but now he felt a big lump come into his throat, and hot tears ran down his cheeks. His wonderful *NO PROBLEM* T-shirt! It was gone for ever. He would never see it again.

They did not have to wait long at the airport before their flight was called. 'That's us,' Dad said, standing up. 'Come on, Davy.'

They joined a queue of people at the door. Their plane was standing on the runway outside.

Just then, there was a commotion behind them. Davy heard loud voices speaking in fast Greek, then a voice called, 'Davy!'

It was Spiro.

Davy ran back towards the door. Spiro was smiling widely. 'You forgot something,' he said, pushing the T-shirt into Davy's hands. He had driven all the way to the airport in his car especially to give Davy his shirt.

'Come on, Davy. Hurry up!' Dad called. Everyone else had gone to the plane.

Spiro gave him a little push. 'Don't miss your plane!' he said.

'Thank you for bringing my shirt, Spiro. Thanks a lot.'

'That's all right. But you do something for me, Davy-mou.'

'What's that?' Davy was curious.

'You come back to Corfu again next year,' Spiro told him, and Davy grinned.

'No problem, Spiro,' he chuckled. 'No problem!'

5
The Bird Hospital

'What have you got there?' asked Davy one sunny Saturday morning.

He peered between the wooden boards of the fence, trying to see what Mrs Next-Door was holding in her hands. (Mrs Next-Door's real name was Mrs Feasby-Gamble but that was hard to remember.)

Mrs Next-Door looked very sad. 'It's a blackbird,' she told him. 'Snowy caught it in the garden.'

Snowy, Mrs Next-Door's cat, was always chasing birds, but usually they flew away while Snowy was still running across the lawn.

'Is the blackbird dead?' asked Davy.

'No—and it doesn't look hurt, either. It's had a nasty shock, though, and it needs looking after. I wish I knew what to do with it.'

'No problem,' said Davy straight away. 'We'll look after it. My dad won't mind. He once set a bird's broken leg and it mended OK. He's a good bird doctor, my dad.'

Very gently, Davy carried the bird indoors. It lay quite still in his hands. Mum and Dad both looked at it and said perhaps it just needed a long rest. Dad put some cotton-wool into a cardboard box and made a soft bed for the bird.

He put the bird's hospital-box on a shelf in the shed where it was dark and quiet. Davy was so excited about the bird that he didn't want to go shopping in the town with Mum, even though they would be stopping for burgers and French fries. But she made him go anyway as he needed new shoes.

As they walked from shop to shop, Davy kept thinking about the blackbird.

Davy had never owned a pet of his own, so he was thrilled about the bird. It would be his very first pet. When it got well again he'd ask Dad to buy a cage for it, like Grandma's budgie.

Grandma West's budgie, Dixie, lived in a cage. It was a very clever bird—it could say 'Little Miss Muffet sat on a tuffet'. Only sometimes it got mixed up and said 'Little Miss Tuffet sat on a muffet', and that made Davy laugh.

When the blackbird was better, he thought, he would teach it to talk like Dixie. It would learn to perch on his shoulder like the parrot in his *Blackbeard the Pirate* book. The blackbird would ride to school on his shoulder and he'd show it to Miss Croft, his teacher.

Davy was so eager to get home that he agreed on the first pair of shoes he tried on instead of saying he didn't like them, which was what usually happened when he went to buy shoes.

As soon as they got home, he dashed through the gate, up the drive and round to the back of the house.

'Is the bird better?' he said, bursting in through the kitchen door. He stopped when he saw his dad's face. The smile-lines were still there, around his mouth, but the smile had gone.

He shook his head. 'It won't eat or drink anything, Davy,' he said. 'It must be more hurt than we thought.'

'Can I see it?' asked Davy. Dad went out to the shed with him and gently lifted the hospital-box off the shelf. Davy looked at the bird.

It was so still that, for a minute, Davy thought it was dead. Then he saw the little chest rise up and down. He stroked its head gently with one finger. The dark feathers felt very soft.

'Will it die?' Davy asked his dad. There was a

lump in his throat and he had to whisper the words.

'I don't know, son. Maybe.' Dad put the box back on the shelf.

Davy stared hard at the shed wall, trying hard to swallow the lump. 'I don't want it to die, Dad,' he said at last. 'I want it for a pet. If it got better we could buy a cage for it and teach it to say nursery rhymes like Dixie.'

Dad held Davy's hand very tight. Davy could tell he was thinking hard.

'Blackbirds are wild birds, Davy,' Dad said at last. 'They like to live in trees and look for worms in the garden. It wouldn't be fair to put it into a cage.'

'But Dixie lives in a cage,' Davy reminded him.

'Dixie is a budgie. He's lived in a cage since he was an egg,' said Dad. 'He's used to it.'

'The blackbird could get used to it.'

Dad lifted Davy up to sit on his workbench among the curly wood shavings, where he could see out of the window. He could see his roller skates lying on the drive, and his bike leaning against a tree, and the lawn that ran right down to the edge of the road.

'How would you feel, Davy, if someone took you and shut you up inside a little room, and never let you go out to play? You could never go to school, or ride your bike, or go to Uncle Alan's to play with Tessa and her puppies.'

Davy thought he wouldn't like it much. He would especially miss playing with Tessa's puppies.

They'd been born a few weeks ago, and they were all fat and warm and wriggly. There was one special pup that always ran to meet Davy. It had a big black patch over one ear. It would be horrid never to be able to see it again.

He knew what Dad meant. The blackbird would feel sad if it was made to live in a cage. He pictured the bird flying freely around the garden, where it belonged.

That night, when he said his prayers, Davy added a sentence.

'Please, God,' he prayed, 'make the blackbird get well again so it can go back to live in the trees. Amen.'

Davy went to sleep thinking of the bird. Now he'd asked God about it, it would surely get better.

He remembered the time last winter when he'd lost his gloves at school. He prayed extra hard about the gloves because they were new ones and he knew his mum would be very cross when she found out he'd lost them.

Miss Croft had helped him to look for them—and there the gloves were, on the floor under the bench in the cloakroom.

So Davy knew, because of the gloves—and other things as well—that God always answers when you pray about things.

The next day was Sunday. Davy leapt out of bed as soon as he woke up and ran downstairs and out to the shed in his pyjamas to see if the bird was better.

The box had gone from the shelf.

Davy went slowly indoors again. He went upstairs to his mum and dad's bedroom. Both of them were there, fast asleep. He could hear Amy chattering to herself in baby language in her cot in the next room.

Davy shook his dad's shoulder.

'Whasamarrer?' His dad rolled over, talking sleepy-language. Davy knew that meant, 'What's the matter?'

'My bird's gone,' Davy said in a small voice.

His dad opened one eye, then the other.

'The box isn't on the shelf in the shed.'

Dad sat up and swung both legs out of bed.

He took Davy's hand and they walked downstairs to the kitchen together. 'The blackbird was very ill, Davy,' Dad said. 'It died last night.'

Davy's eyes filled with tears. How could his bird be dead? He had asked God to make it better!

At last, Davy found his voice. 'But I asked God to make it better. That's not fair!'

'If you asked me for some sweets and I said "No", that wouldn't mean I hadn't answered you, would it? God always answers us, Davy. Sometimes he says "Yes" and sometimes he asks us to wait a while. But sometimes it's wiser for him to say "No". We don't always understand.'

Davy slid off his chair, feeling sad inside. He understood what Dad had said now. But he still wished God had been able to say 'Yes'.

That afternoon Mum took Davy and Amy to the park. When they got home Davy ran in through the kitchen door—then stopped in surprise.

There, in a box in the corner, was one of Tessa's puppies. The pup looked at Davy then flopped itself over the side of the box and waddled across to meet him. It was his favourite—the one with the black patch on its ear.

Dad nodded, smiling. 'Uncle Alan didn't tell you before, but he's been keeping Patch especially for you.'

Patch. It was the perfect name for him. Davy stroked and patted Patch, fondling his floppy ears.

'You'll have to learn to look after him properly, though,' Dad went on. 'You must feed him and take him out for walks every day and teach him to be

good. Having a dog is harder work than you think!'

Davy nodded. He would be the very best master there was. 'Here, Patch,' he said, and the fat puppy lolloped up to him again as if he already knew his name, wagging his tail so hard that his bottom wagged to and fro as well. Davy laughed in delight.

With a pang of sadness, he thought about the bird, and he knew that God had done what was best for it.

Patch squatted suddenly and made a little wet puddle on the kitchen floor. Davy pulled a face.

'Bad dog!' he said firmly. 'That kind of thing has to be done in the garden!'

He picked the puppy up and headed for the door—then stopped and looked back at the puddle. He sighed. Dad was right—having a dog wasn't going to be easy. He hadn't thought of having to mop up puddles. 'But I suppose *this* is part of looking after you properly!' he said.

And Davy opened the cupboard under the sink, took out a floorcloth, and set to work.

6

If Only . . .

It was Davy's cousin Tom's birthday. He was going to be eight on Saturday.

On Tuesday after school, Davy and Mum went to the shops together, and Davy picked a present for Tom all by himself—an utterly brilliant police helicopter with rotors that whizzed round and round with the whop, whop, whop sound of a real helicopter. He knew Tom would like it, because he himself would have given anything to own a helicopter like that.

He watched as Mum emptied her shopping bag on to the table. There were some groceries for old Mrs Walker, who lived around the corner. Mum did shopping for her because the old lady couldn't walk properly without a stick. Then Mum put her own groceries away in the kitchen cupboard, and firmly put Tom's present in the top cupboard.

When Dad got home from work, Mum took the helicopter out of its box and showed it to him.

'Can I look at it?' asked Davy, and Mum held it out for him to see. But that wasn't what Davy meant. He wanted to hold it himself, to switch it on, to see the rotors go round, to run around the room with it, pretending the police were on their way to catch a gang of bank robbers.

'Can I hold it?'

Mum shook her head. 'Sorry, Davy, but I don't want it to get broken, and it might if I let you play with it now.'

She carefully put the helicopter back inside its box, then opened the cupboard door and put the box high up on the top shelf.

'Why don't you take Patch out to play?' Dad suggested. 'He hasn't been out for a run today.'

Davy took Patch into the garden. They played games—but Davy couldn't forget about the helicopter. He threw sticks across the lawn and Patch brought them back to him again. Still Davy thought about the helicopter. If only he could play with it, just for a few minutes. It wasn't fair. Mum always thought he was going to break things.

Mum called Davy in for his tea. She had made a ham and pineapple pizza—Davy's favourite—and there were baked potatoes and peas too.

After tea, Dad went out to his workbench in the

garage. He was making a toybox for Davy. Mum put on her coat, and dressed little sister Amy in hers.

'I'm going around to Mrs Walker's with her groceries,' Mum said. 'Do you want to come with me?'

The old lady kept a tin of sweets especially for when Davy called in to see her. He nearly said 'Yes'—then shook his head.

'I'd rather read my book,' he said.

'All right,' Mum said. She ruffled his hair as she walked past him. 'I'll be back soon. Behave yourself.'

From the window, Davy watched her walk down the driveway and along the street. She saw Davy watching and waved to him. She moved Amy's hand up and down, too, teaching her to wave. Davy waved back.

When she had gone, Davy didn't read his book. He opened the cupboard door and looked up at the top shelf. He could just see the blue edge of the helicopter box. His heart was thumping very hard. He knew he ought not to touch the box —but he knew he was going to.

After all, he asked himself, what harm would it do? No problem! He was only going to take the helicopter out of the box and hold it in his hand for a minute. How would that break it? Even if he switched it on it wouldn't really matter. It was meant to be switched on, wasn't it? Toys were meant to be played with.

Davy dragged a dining chair across the room and climbed up on it. He stood on tiptoe and lifted the box out of the cupboard. He opened the box and slid the helicopter out of it.

It was one of the best things Davy had ever seen. He wished it was his own birthday instead of Tom's. His finger found the switch, and he pushed it. Whop, whop, whop went the fast-spinning rotors, and Davy held the helicopter above his head and circled it slowly.

'Control to Charlie Victor Four ... Robbery at the High Street Bank ... All cars in the area please attend. Ten-four. Stand by ...'

Slam went the garage door. Davy heard heavy footsteps walking down the side of the house. Dad was coming.

Davy's heart started to beat very fast. His mouth went suddenly dry. His hands shook as he flicked the switch off, grabbed the box and crammed the helicopter inside. Hurry, Hurry.

Click went the handle of the back door.

Davy fumbled with the end flap of the box. The box slid from his fingers.

Crash! Down it went on to the floor. A rotor blade flew out of the box and broke in half. Davy froze on his chair, appalled at what he had done.

He heard Dad go into the kitchen and turn the tap on. He whistled a tune as he washed his hands. Davy jumped from the chair, scooped up the broken bits, shoved them into the box, then pushed the box back on to the shelf in the cupboard. Then he dragged the chair back into its place by the table.

When Dad came into the room Davy was curled up in an armchair, his book on his knee. Dad didn't notice that Davy's breathing was faster than usual.

That evening was awful. For the first time he could remember in the whole of his life, Davy couldn't wait for bedtime to come. He didn't want to play with his cars or watch television or take Patch for a walk. He was feeling sick inside. He couldn't think about anything else except the broken helicopter.

Mum and Dad would find out. Davy knew they would—they always seemed to know when he had done something he shouldn't. He could never understand how they knew—but they always did.

And even if Mum wrapped up the box for Tom without looking inside it, Tom would tell them straight away that the helicopter was broken.

And what about Tom? How disappointed he would be to open his birthday parcel and find a broken helicopter inside. What a rotten birthday present.

Davy squirmed on his chair. Oh—if only he'd never touched it. If only he'd listened to his mum. If only he'd done as he was told. If only . . .

Davy knew he ought to tell her what he had done, but he was scared. He didn't want her to know . . . But she would know anyway . . .

Horrible thoughts went round and round inside his head, and he couldn't stop them.

Wednesday went by, then Thursday. Still Mum didn't look at the helicopter. On Friday, she went to the corner shop and bought some wrapping paper with blue and red cars on it. She took the helicopter box out of the cupboard. Davy couldn't bear to watch, so he took Patch out into the garden. He sat still on the swing, waiting for her to shout. She did.

'Davy, Davy, come here—I want you!'

Davy swallowed hard. He went back inside, his

heart pounding so hard he thought she must see it moving up and down under his jumper.

Mum looked up as he went into the room. She spoke sternly. 'Davy—have you been playing with this helicopter?'

Here was his chance to tell her the truth and say that he was sorry. But instead, he shook his head.

'No. Why?'

She held out the broken pieces. 'This is why, Davy.' Davy looked at the toy. Not only was a rotor blade broken but a window had fallen out too.

Mum went on: 'It wasn't broken when I looked at it last and, as far as I know, toys don't break themselves. Now, Davy, I want the truth. You took it out of the cupboard, didn't you?'

He shook his head again. 'No, of course not. It wasn't me.' Davy thought fast. 'Perhaps it got knocked when you pushed it on to the shelf.'

'Oh, Davy,' Mum said, slowly. She looked sad, and her eyes were very bright. Surely Mum couldn't be crying?

Davy turned away. There was a tight feeling across his chest. He tried to whistle as if he didn't care, but found himself blowing through dry lips.

'It was you, wasn't it, Davy?'

Davy swallowed a lump in his throat, then slowly nodded. 'I'm sorry. It was an accident, Mum. I didn't break it on purpose.' Tears spilled

over on to his cheeks and he wiped them away with the back of his hand.

'Of course you didn't. But you took it out of the cupboard on purpose, didn't you?'

Davy knew he had. He looked down at his feet and said nothing.

Mum gave a heavy sigh. 'You played with the helicopter after I'd said you couldn't; that was bad enough. But pretending you didn't know anything about it makes it twice as bad.'

Davy hadn't thought of that before. But he thought of it now, and the sadness inside him was like a big heavy weight in his tummy. 'I'm ... I'm sorry,' he whispered.

'Good.' Mum put out a hand and tipped his chin upwards until he was looking at her. 'But the next time you know that you've done something wrong, be brave enough to admit it,' she said.

Davy was sent to bed straight away, without any tea. He didn't think he could have eaten any anyway, he felt so bad inside. But as an extra punishment, Mum made Davy open his china savings pig with the slot in its back, and take out enough money to buy another present for Tom.

There was no time now to go into town to the big shops to buy another helicopter, so Mum got a red fire engine from the corner shop.

'I'm sorry, Mum,' he told her as he watched her wrap it up in the coloured wrapping paper. 'I'll never do anything like that again.'

She put an arm right around him and hugged him close. 'That's good,' she whispered. 'I'm glad.'

Davy felt better. It was good to know that however bad he was, Mum still loved him. He passed her the sticky tape and she sealed up the parcel. Then she wrote Tom's name on a little card and stuck it on the top.

Davy sighed. He felt happier now—but deep down inside he was still a little bit sad.

The fire engine was all right. But he knew that Tom would rather have had the shiny police helicopter with rotors that spun round and round.

7

Have You Seen My Dog?

Mum was cutting sandwiches. In the middle of the table was a pile of tomatoes, crisp packets and shiny green apples.

'We're going out for a picnic!' Davy cried, and Dad grinned at him.

'Yes. We didn't tell you yesterday in case it was raining this morning and we couldn't go. You'd have been disappointed then.' He took a big bottle of lemonade out of the fridge and put it into a brown and white picnic cool box, then piled in all the other food.

Davy liked going out. 'Where are we going?' he asked eagerly.

'Rocklands Park,' Dad told him, still smiling widely.

'Rocklands Park—great!' shouted Davy.

Davy had been there once before, so he knew that Rocklands Park was a brilliant place. There was a big lake with boats you could row. There was a playground that had swings and roundabouts and a tall helter-skelter. And best of all there was a butterfly farm, which was like an enormous greenhouse where hundreds of different coloured butterflies flew among the trees and flowers that had been planted alongside little streams and waterfalls.

They set off as soon as they had finished breakfast. Mum fastened Amy into her car safety seat. Davy clipped on his seat belt. Patch jumped on to the back seat next to Davy, his tongue hanging out and his tail wagging madly to and fro. He loved riding in the car.

Davy wanted to see the butterflies first, so when they arrived they left Patch in the car. Dogs couldn't go to butterfly farms, Dad said. It was a sunny day, so they parked in the shade and left the car windows open a little way to give the puppy some fresh air.

'We won't be long, Patch,' Davy told him. But Patch wanted to come too. He whined and pawed at the window.

'We'll take him with us later,' said Dad.

The butterflies were beautiful. They looked just like red, blue and yellow flower. petals fluttering among the green trees.

'Pretty!' Mum told Amy, pointing. 'Look at the pretty butterflies, Amy.' And Amy stretched out a small hand as if she was trying to catch one.

Patch was glad to see them when they got back to the car. Even with the windows open it was quite hot inside. Next to the car park was a picnic area with wooden tables and benches. Dad got the cool box out of the car boot and they sat at one of the tables and ate their lunch. Mum had brought Patch's bowl and a bottle of water. She poured some out for him, and he drank it all straight away.

'Can we go to the playground now?' asked Davy, gathering up the crisp bags and sandwich wrappers. He put them all into the bin that stood by the gateway.

The playground wasn't far away. But there was a big notice on the gate that said: NO DOGS ALLOWED.

'Oh, dear,' said Mum. 'We can't take Patch in here, either.'

'It's too hot now to leave him in the car,' Dad said.

There was an iron post next to the gate. 'We could tie his lead to the post,' Mum suggested. 'He'll be all right. We can keep coming back to see him.'

And that, to Patch's disappointment, was what they did. He barked after them as they went through the gate. 'We'll be back,' Davy told him.

They had a wonderful time. Mum sat on the merry-go-round with Amy on her knee. Davy thought the helter-skelter was best. He liked lying on his tummy and whizzing round and round and down and down until he reached the bottom. Then he ran back up the wooden staircase and started all over again.

Mum and Dad took Amy on the see-saw. Mum sat at one end and Dad sat at the other with Amy in front of him.

'I'm going to see if Patch is all right,' Davy called to them. Patch was his dog, and it was his job to look after him.

'All right,' said his dad. 'But don't untie his lead from the post. Just check that he's all right, then come straight back.'

Davy ran to the gate. Patch was pleased to see him. He jumped up at Davy, licking him all over and barking loudly and pulling frantically against his lead.

Davy sat down on the ground and put his arms around the wriggling Patch. Patch licked his face and whined. It seemed as if he was saying, 'Where have you been all this time?'

'I'm sorry we had to leave you alone,' Davy told
him. 'But you see, dogs aren't allowed in the
playground.'

Patch whined again, straining on the lead. 'You
want a little run around, don't you?' said Davy.

He remembered what his dad had said about not untying the lead from the post. But what difference was it going to make? He would just let him have a little run, then tie him back up again. No problem. Dogs needed to run around, didn't they? He reached out and unclipped the lead.

Free at last, Patch jumped up at Davy, then ran joyfully round and round in circles.

'That's better, isn't it, boy?' Davy said.

'Woof!' said Patch.

'Woof!' said another doggy voice from the other side of the road.

A little brown spaniel was glaring across at them, showing its teeth. Patch's head swung round, and his tail went down as he saw the spaniel. He growled.

The two dogs rushed towards each other.

'Patch, come here!' shouted Davy.

But Patch took no notice. Snapping and snarling, the two fighting dogs rolled together on the ground.

'Jingo!' a man shouted to the spaniel. 'Stop that at once, do you hear me? Come here!' But the dogs went on fighting.

The man had a walking stick. He struck out at the dogs with the stick and they sprang apart. He grabbed his own dog by the collar, but Patch dodged Davy's hand and dashed away down the road as fast as he could go. Davy stared after him in horror.

'Davy—what's going on?'

Davy turned round. He had been such a long time that his dad and mum had come looking for him.

'It's Patch, Dad!' Davy cried. 'He's run off!'

Dad looked at him sternly. 'How could he run off when his lead was tied to the post?'

'I thought he needed a run, Dad,' Davy told him. 'I was going to fasten him up again, honestly. It was that other dog's fault. It started barking at Patch, and then they started fighting.'

'Was it really the dog's fault?' Mum asked him quietly.

Davy pushed a stone about with the toe of his shoe. He knew it was his fault, not the dog's.

'If you had done as you were told, this wouldn't have happened, would it? Now Patch is lost in a strange town.'

'I'm sorry,' said Davy.

'We'd better walk around and try to find him,' said Dad. 'I wonder where he's got to?'

Patch, at that moment, was on his way across a football pitch. He liked playing football. As the big black and white ball came hurtling towards him, the little dog jumped up to meet it and headed the ball, just as he did when he played with Davy.

'Gerrout, dog!' Patch looked up and saw a fierce and very solid boy racing across the field towards him, head down.

After one look at the tough-looking boy, he decided that football wasn't his game after all.

He trotted back through the gate. Then he ran down the street until he came to a row of houses. He went through another gate and into a yard. A white cloth was spread out in the middle of the yard, and around it sat five dolls and a small girl. Patch put his head on one side and watched as the little girl set out six plates and carefully laid one biscuit on each plate.

He gave a short 'Wuff', and wagged his tail.

'You want a biscuit, dog, don't you?' said the little girl.

Patch did. He sat up on his hind legs as Davy had taught him, and begged for a biscuit. She threw him one. He gobbled it down at once, then waited for another.

'These are for my dollies,' she told Patch.

When he saw she wasn't going to give him any more he went back out of the gate and down the street.

A few doors further along, a man was washing his car. Patch ran up to watch, wagging his tail. The man reached into his bucket and took out a soapy sponge.

'Watch out, dog,' he said, and Patch jumped back as soapy drops splashed around him. He shook himself and trotted on.

Patch was getting hungry. The biscuit had only filled a tiny corner, so when he smelled something good cooking he followed his nose and went through a gate into another yard.

The kitchen door stood open and a fat woman in a blue checked overall was cooking chops in a frying pan. Patch put his nose through the door and gave a short, sharp bark. The woman looked up and saw him.

'Out!' she shouted, raising her hand. In it was a long-handled wooden spoon. 'No dogs allowed in here!'

Patch turned tail and ran.

A few doors further along, a white cat was sitting on a low wall.

Patch liked cats. He could never understand

why they always ran away from him.

'Woof!' he said to the cat. The cat hissed at him, then turned and ran. Patch followed.

But he soon lost interest in the cat. The little dog was feeling hot and tired. If only he could find somewhere nice and cool, where he could lie down and have a nap.

The kitchen door of this house was open also, but Patch didn't make the mistake of going in. He might get chased again.

Next to the kitchen door was another door which stood slightly open. Patch nosed his way inside. Oh, wonderful! The tiny room was cool and dark and quiet. Patch lay down, and before long he was fast asleep. And when the door closed with a sharp click, he simply turned over and went back to sleep ...

'I wonder where he can be,' said Davy unhappily.

His dog was gone, and it was his fault. 'Please, God,' he whispered, 'please let us find him.' If they could only find Patch, he'd always do as he was told in future ... At least, he would try.

They stopped by a football field. 'Perhaps someone here has seen him,' said Dad.

Davy asked a man who was watching the match. The man laughed. 'A black and white dog? Why, yes. He was trying to join in the game. He ran back out of the gate, though.'

They walked on down the street. A little girl nursing a doll sat on a wall outside a house.

'Have you seen my dog?' asked Davy. 'He's black and white.'

The little girl nodded. 'He came to my tea party,' she told Davy. 'He ate a biscuit.'

They walked on. A man was waxing his car, polishing it hard with a cloth until it shone brightly.

'Have you seen my black and white dog?' asked Davy.

'Yes—he got sprayed with soapy water when I was washing my car,' the man chuckled.

They walked on. A woman carrying a shopping bag came out of a house. 'Have you seen my dog?' asked Davy.

'A black and white one?' said the woman. 'Yes, I certainly have—it would have stolen my chops if I'd given it half a chance!'

They walked on. There was nobody else in sight. After a minute Mum said, 'Do you hear something?'

'What kind of something?'

'Listen . . .'

Then they all heard it. It was faint and far away, but it was a dog barking.

'It's a dog,' said Dad.

'It's Patch!' cried Davy. So God had answered another prayer; this time, he'd said 'yes'!

They all ran round to the back of the house. A white cat watched them from the roof of a shed.

The barking was coming from behind a closed door. Dad didn't like opening other people's doors, so he knocked on the kitchen door first. There was no reply.

'They must be out,' said Mum.

Davy could wait no longer. He lifted the catch of the door and Patch bounded out. But what a changed Patch! Instead of being black and white he had turned black and dark grey.

Mum and Dad both backed away from him. 'It's coal dust,' said Dad. 'This is a coal store!'

'Into the bath with him, the minute we get home!' Mum said, looking at the dog in horror. He was filthy!

But Davy didn't care what colour his dog was. He darted forward, his arms outstretched, and the excited little dog jumped right into them, licking

Davy's face as if he hadn't seen him for a year. 'Davy—just look at yourself!' Mum exclaimed. 'Now you're as black as the dog!'

But Davy just grinned up at her, his pink mouth wide in his dirt-smeared face. 'We'll both need a bath the minute we get home, won't we?' he said.

He clipped the dog's lead back on to his collar.

'Come on Patch,' he said. 'Let's go ... and I'll race you to the bathroom!'

8
Buried Treasure

Davy was in trouble again. But this time, Davy himself had nothing to do with the trouble he was in.

It was a warm summer Saturday morning a few days before Grandma West's birthday. Mum had carried Amy's playpen outside into the back garden so that she could play safely and get some fresh air at the same time. And Mum was sitting next to the playpen in the sunshine, sewing, her needle flashing in and out of the material.

She was sewing a picture for Grandma's birthday. It was a little cottage in a garden of beautiful flowers, with a black and white dog running up the garden path. Davy liked the picture because the dog was just like Patch. When you looked at it very closely it was all made from tiny crosses that Mum was putting in with her needle and coloured thread. When it was finished, the picture was going to be put into a frame and given to

Grandma West on her birthday.

Davy was looking forward to Grandma West's birthday. He had already spent a whole week's pocket money at the corner shop, where he had bought her a beautiful purple ring.

Davy didn't know how old she was going to be. He had asked her, but she only said, 'I'm as old as my tongue and a good deal older than my teeth,' which told Davy nothing at all. He only knew she must be very old indeed as her teeth were pink and white plastic ones instead of proper ones like his own, and she had wriggly veins on the backs of her hands, and aching bones, too. And she called the radio a 'wireless', just like old Mrs Walker did.

And now on this sunny Saturday morning everyone was outside in the sunshine. Everyone, that is, except Davy. Davy was watching a cartoon on television.

'Come outside in the sunshine, Davy,' Mum called, her head bent over her work. 'It's such a lovely day, it's a shame to waste it by sitting indoors.'

Davy didn't answer. If he kept quiet, he thought, she might forget that she'd told him to go outside. He didn't want to go out and miss the rest of the programme.

'Davy—do you hear me? Switch off the television now. You've watched it for long enough.'

Davy wriggled right down into his chair. Still he didn't answer.

Mum sighed, stood up and put her sewing down on the chair. She went into the house. 'Davy—did you hear what I said? I told you to come outside. You can watch television another time.'

'I don't want to watch it another time.' There was a whine in Davy's voice. 'I want to watch it now.' It was his favourite programme.

Mum crossed the room and flicked off the switch.

'Don't. Oh, Mum!'

'Outside,' she said.

Davy balled his hands into fists and shoved them hard down into his pockets. It wasn't fair. He didn't want to play outside. He stalked out of the room and into the garden. He kicked a stone as hard as he could. It whizzed into the air and bounced off the fence, and Mrs Next-Door's cat, watching him from behind a bush, scooted away.

He sat down on the grass. 'Boring. Boring. Boring,' he muttered to himself. There was nothing to do out here.

Patch ran up with his chewed-up old ball and dropped it at Davy's feet.

'Go away, Patch. I don't feel like playing ball just now,' he said. Patch snuffled at the ball, then began to chew on it again. The puppy was growing into a very chewy dog.

Then he heard the front door bell chime. 'Who can that be?' he heard his mother say as she stood up again. 'Keep an eye on Amy for me, will you, Davy, while I go and answer the door?'

Amy was playing with her kelly doll. The doll, which had a clown's face, was round underneath instead of having legs, and when anyone knocked it over it rolled around then stood straight up again. Davy leaned into the playpen and held the doll flat on the ground. Amy was not pleased. She looked up at him, her bottom lip trembling. He let go, and the doll flipped upwards at top speed, then rocked frantically to and fro. Amy laughed. He did it again, and again. Soon Amy was chuckling loudly.

After a few minutes, Mum came outside again. 'Who was at the door?' Davy wanted to know.

'The window cleaner called for his pay—I was out last time he cleaned the windows.' She looked around, hunting for something. 'Davy—have you seen my sewing?'

'No,' Davy told her.

She looked at him doubtfully. 'But it was right here on the chair.'

'Perhaps you took it indoors with you.'

'I can't have done,' she said—but she went to look anyway. She came back empty-handed.

'I've looked everywhere, and I can't find it. I put it down on the chair when I went to answer the door. I know I did.' Her voice became hard and cross. 'Davy—you must know something about it. You were the only one here, apart from Amy—and I'm sure she didn't jump out of her playpen, hide my sewing, then jump back in again.'

Davy shook his head. 'But I didn't do anything. Honestly, Mum. I've been playing with Amy's doll ever since you went inside. I don't know where it is.'

Mum pressed her lips together until they became a thin line.

'Honestly,' said Davy.

She didn't believe him. He knew he hadn't seen the sewing, but she didn't believe him.

'I wish I could believe you, Davy,' she said, almost as if she could read his thoughts. 'But there's nobody else here who could have taken it. Please, tell me the truth. You were angry with me, weren't you, for turning off the television and making you come outside? You were angry, and you decided to get even with me by hiding my sewing.'

Davy was shaking his head. 'No!' he said. 'No, I didn't touch it. Why won't you believe me?'

'Perhaps I'd find it easier to believe you, Davy, if you'd always told me the truth,' she said.

Davy pursed his lips and said nothing. He got up and stalked angrily down the garden path between the rows of cabbages and broad beans and round to the back of the toolshed. Davy's den was here; he had made it by leaning a row of planks against the shed wall. He crawled inside his den on hands and knees.

Still feeling angry inside, he opened the old biscuit tin full of cars he kept there, took out his green lorry, slowly piled it up with tiny stones, then ran it to and fro across the ground. His heart wasn't in the game, though.

Why wouldn't his mother believe him? He wanted the picture to be finished in time for Grandma's birthday just as much as she did. It wasn't fair. She was always picking on him ... and when he was telling the truth, too.

But you don't always tell her the truth, do you?

The quiet voice inside his mind startled Davy, and he sat quite still, gripping the tractor tightly in his hand.

Dad had told him about the quiet voice inside that would help him to know what was right and what was wrong. He called it his conscience. Was this it?

Dad said it was hard to do what your conscience said was right, such as telling the truth when it was easier to tell a lie. Sometimes, telling the truth got you into trouble. But if he talked to

God about it, God would help him to do the right thing, even when it was hard.

Davy remembered Tom's broken helicopter. No, he hadn't always told her the truth. He knew he hadn't touched her sewing—but how could Mum know whether he was telling the truth or not, if sometimes he told the truth and sometimes he told lies?

He opened the biscuit tin and put the lorry back inside. It must be nearly lunchtime . . . he would go back and help her to get it ready. He would lay the table and get out the glasses and the salt and pepper pots. Perhaps, then, she would see that he was being good. And when she found the sewing—wherever she had put it—she would see for herself that this time he was telling the truth.

But things didn't turn out to be as easy as that, because she didn't find the sewing.

After lunch Mum hunted everywhere, even looking in silly places where she knew quite well the sewing couldn't possibly be. And Davy and Dad looked too. But it was no good. It seemed that that piece of sewing had vanished into the air.

It was a real mystery. The sewing had gone, it seemed, for ever.

Mum and Dad bought Grandma West a dark

green cardigan for her birthday instead of giving her the picture. And as time went by, everybody forgot all about it.

The summer days got shorter and cooler. The leaves on the trees once more turned gold and then fell to the ground to make a crisp, brown carpet.

In the garden, all the vegetables had been picked and eaten a long time ago. All that was left were rows of withered pea and bean stems.

One fine Saturday, Dad took his fork and his spade out of the toolshed and began to tidy up the garden before winter came. He broke off all the dried-up stems and threw them on to the compost heap. Then he began to dig ...

Davy, wearing a big apron tied around his middle, was in the kitchen making chocolate crispies, carefully stirring cornflakes into a big bowl of melted chocolate. Mum was baking a sponge cake.

Suddenly, Dad opened the back door and came into the kitchen. One hand was hidden behind his back. He held out the other hand so that Mum and Davy could see. In it was a torn and dirty piece of material.

'Look what I've found!' he said.

The piece of sewing was black with garden soil,

but both Davy and Mum knew what it was straight away.

'My needlework!' Mum cried. 'But where did you find it?'

'It was buried in the garden,' Dad said, chuckling, 'like a real buried treasure.'

'Buried in the garden!' echoed Mum. 'But how on earth did it get there?' She turned and looked at Davy. 'You didn't...'

'No, Mum, I didn't,' said Davy.

'No, he didn't,' said Dad, and he was laughing now.

'How do you know it wasn't me?' Davy was curious. How could Dad tell?

'Because of this.' And Dad took his other hand from behind his back. In it was Patch's chewed up old ball.

'Patch was working hard at burying things, the day the sewing disappeared,' Dad said. 'He must have run off with the picture when Mum went to answer the door. He took it down the garden and played with it for a while—probably while we were all busy searching for it. Then, when he got tired, he simply buried it along with his favourite things. There was a smelly old bone buried there, too.'

Davy's mum sat down with a plop on to a kitchen chair. She looked again at the sewing. Then she looked at Davy. She seemed dazed.

'I just don't know what to say,' she said.

'I knew it wasn't me,' said Davy.

'Of course you knew. And I'm sorry, Davy, that I didn't believe you. I really should have known you were telling the truth. But ...'

'I know,' said Davy before she could say any more. He had a big smile on his face. 'Once you start telling lies, people don't know when you're telling the truth!'

Mum smiled down at Davy, and he knew she trusted him again.

And, Davy decided, it was good to be trusted.

9
Hot Cross Bunnies

Davy was excited. His Uncle Jim, who was a sailor on a big ship, was coming home from the sea to spend Christmas at their house.

Uncle Jim had been at sea for so long that Davy had only seen him once before, and that didn't count because he had been too little to remember.

Davy had seen photographs of him, of course. And Mum and Dad had talked about him—especially Mum, as Uncle Jim was her brother.

But now, at long last, his sailor uncle was really coming home. And what was more, he was coming home in time for Christmas, and that made it even more exciting.

On the day Uncle Jim was to arrive, Mum and Dad put a folding bed in Davy's room for Uncle Jim to sleep on. They were going to have an extra special dinner of roast beef and Yorkshire pudding, and Grandma West was coming for the day too.

'You'll like Uncle Jim,' Mum told Davy as she

stirred gravy in a pan on the hob. 'He's always full of fun, and he tells jokes all the time. *And* he can waggle his ears.'

Grandma West frowned and pursed up her lips. She did that, Davy knew, when something happened that she wasn't pleased about. 'Jim tells far too many jokes,' she said sternly. 'It's high time he learnt that life is a serious matter.'

Soon Davy's tummy was rumbling. The table was laid and the dinner was ready. But Uncle Jim hadn't come.

'We'll start without him,' said Mum, sighing.

They ate their roast beef and Yorkshire pudding, and Uncle Jim still hadn't come. Mum covered his dinner with cling-film and put it in the fridge. 'It'll warm up later,' she said.

Grandma got out her knitting. Little sister Amy woke up from her nap and Mum gave her her lunch.

Davy waited. He played with the Transformer robots he had been given last Christmas, and wondered what this year's presents would be. He watched a cartoon on television. He tidied up the cars in his toy garage. Still Uncle Jim hadn't come.

Davy sighed. 'Perhaps he's not coming after all.'

'He'll come,' said Mum. 'You'll just have to be patient.'

Dad came home from work, and Uncle Jim hadn't come. Dad let Davy stay up late to wait for him, but when he fell asleep with his head on Grandma West's wide lap, Mum woke him up and made him go to bed.

'It's not fair,' Davy grumbled as he got into his pyjamas and climbed into bed. 'Why can't I stay up until he comes? I want to see him waggle his ears.'

'It's late, Davy.' Mum gave him a goodnight kiss and tucked the covers around him. 'You'll see Uncle Jim and his ears tomorrow.'

Davy sat up again as she went out of the room. 'I won't be able to go to sleep again,' he called after her.

But he did. He didn't hear the front door bell when it chimed at half past ten, and he slept through the shouting and loud laughter from the hallway below his bedroom.

It was morning. Davy woke up all over at once, as he usually did, and stretched his feet downwards and his arms upwards. He jumped as his hand caught his Mickey Mouse clock on the bedside cabinet and sent it clattering to the floor.

He frowned. That was funny—someone must have moved it. Usually, it was too far away from him to knock it off by accident.

He bent over the edge of the bed, picked up the clock and gave it a little shake. It was still ticking. He put it back on the bedside cabinet—and saw that a man's watch was where the clock usually stood, together with a wallet, a ball-point pen, a toffee and a pile of loose change.

Davy looked across at the low folding bed. Beneath the covers was a humpy shape topped by a tousled mop of very black hair. And just below the hair was a pair of dark eyes, looking at him.

He looked back at the eyes. 'Are you my Uncle Jim?'

'No, I'm Santa Claus,' a muffled voice told him. 'I lost my way in the night and your mum said I could sleep in your Uncle Jim's bed.'

'Huh!' Davy sat up in bed. It's another two weeks to Christmas, and Santa Claus won't be coming until then. So you can't be him. You *are* my Uncle Jim, aren't you? Will you show me how to waggle my ears?'

The man sighed and snuggled further down into the bed. 'At six o'clock in the morning my ears are fast asleep.'

'It's not six, it's seven,' Davy told him. 'I've been able to tell the time for ages. The little hand's on seven and the big hand's on ten. That means it's time to get up.'

'Ten to seven!' Uncle Jim groaned. 'Not on a Saturday morning!'

'Every morning.'

'Well, you go ahead and get up. Then maybe I can get a little sleep!'

In the next room, Amy woke up, rolled over and began to sing cheerfully, as she always did. Through the wall, they heard her. She sang in baby-language and the song was loud and tuneless and didn't sound like any song Uncle Jim had ever heard before. He pulled the blankets up around his ears.

'She doesn't know many real words yet,' Davy told him. 'But she's learning.' He reached out and knocked on the wall, and the singing stopped when he shouted, 'Hello, Amy! Time to get up!'

At the sound of Davy's voice Amy began to jump up and down in excitement, and the cot squeaked and banged as she jumped.

'I've come to a crazy house,' Uncle Jim groaned.

'You'll feel better when you've had a cuppa.' Davy's mum had come into the room, and she was holding out a big mug of tea. 'It's always like this in the mornings, I'm afraid. You'll soon get used to it.'

'Thanks, but I don't think I want to get used to it!'

'I'll help you, Uncle Jim,' Davy promised, and wondered why Uncle Jim groaned again.

After his mug of tea, a shower and a shave, Uncle Jim seemed to be feeling a lot better. He came down to breakfast singing:

> *'Oh, I once knew a girl name Daisy,*
> *And she stood ten feet high,*
> *Her face was painted sky blue pink*
> *And she only had one eye.'*

'That's a good song, Uncle Jim,' said Davy through a mouthful of toast. 'Will you teach it to me?'

'It's not finished yet—there's more.' Uncle Jim went on singing:

> *'With a rom-pom-pom, toodle-ay,*
> *If you'd been there, you'd have laughed all day.*
> *With a rom-pom-pom, toodle-ay,*
> *Early in the morning.'*

Davy laughed. 'With a rom-pom-pom, toodle-ay,' he sang.

'Too-ay, too-ay,' echoed Amy from her high chair.

'Enough!' Mum said sternly. 'Right now, you all eat breakfast. After that you can sing until lunch-time if you want to.'

But there were more exciting things to do. To start with, Uncle Jim waggled his ears for Davy. Davy tried very hard to move his, but his own ears seemed to be stuck fast.

Uncle Jim picked up Davy's football from the outside porch. 'Come on,' he said. 'Let's go down to the playing field and have a game.'

'Great!' said Davy.

Mum made them put on jerseys, coats and scarves as it was very cold.

They played football for a long time. After that they walked down to the shops, where Uncle Jim bought a big bag of liquorice allsorts. Every shop window sparkled with tinsel and Christmas trees, and coloured lights that twinkled red, blue and green.

In the shopping square the crisp air filled with music; a band was playing Christmas carols. A crib had been set up there and Davy and Uncle Jim stopped to look at the lifelike plaster figures of Mary and baby Jesus and Joseph, sitting among the

straw in a stable. A donkey stood by patiently, looking almost real with a piece of hay sticking out of its mouth. The mother, Mary, was rocking her new baby to sleep in her arms.

'Hark! the herald angels sing, Glory to the new-born king,' sang Uncle Jim, joining in the song which the band was playing. Davy sang too, with a warm feeling of gladness inside him, and when he didn't know the words, he sang 'la-la'. Davy just loved Christmas!

'Just think,' said Davy when the song finished. 'If Jesus hadn't been born, we'd never have had Christmas!' He couldn't imagine life without Christmas.

'That's for sure,' Uncle Jim said seriously, looking down at the crib. After a minute he slapped Davy across the shoulders and began to move away. 'Come on,' he said, 'it's time to go home.'

Chewing liquorice allsorts, they walked back from the town centre. And all the time they walked, they talked.

Mum was right. Uncle Jim *was* full of fun. All the way home he told jokes and funny stories.

'What did the Eskimo say when he'd built his new igloo?' Uncle Jim asked Davy.

Davy shook his head. 'Go on, tell me.'

'He said, "Ours is an ice house, ours is."'

Davy frowned as he thought; then he smiled. 'I get it,' he said. 'An ice house—a nice house, right?'

'Right,' said Uncle Jim.

'Now I'll tell you one, Uncle Jim. What smells most in a fish shop?'

'A dead haddock?'

'No—your nose!'

Uncle Jim threw back his head and laughed. Then he said, 'What do you get when you pour hot water down a rabbit-hole?'

'I don't know,' said Davy.

'Hot cross bunnies.'

Davy's forehead creased. 'Hmm,' he said. He'd often eaten hot cross buns—but now he wondered what buns had to do with rabbits.

'Well, the bunnies that lived in the rabbit hole would be hot—and they'd be very cross, too, wouldn't they?'

Davy laughed so hard that he got a pain in his tummy. They were still laughing when they turned into their own street. In the next-door driveway, Oliver was kicking a ball against the garage door. He turned to watch them as they passed by.

'Hi, Oliver,' said Davy, grinning.

'Hi.'

'Is he a friend of yours?' Uncle Jim asked as he followed Davy into the house.

'Sort of . . . he's in my class at school.'

'What a pity we didn't know he was all on his own. He could have come out with us.'

Davy felt guilty suddenly. Oliver was nearly always on his own. He had no brothers or sisters, and not many friends. He didn't even have a dog. Davy was very thoughtful as he took off his coat and scarf.

Grandma West was there, knitting as usual, when they went into the living-room.

'You look frozen,' she said. 'I'll go and put the kettle on.'

'Don't bother,' said Uncle Jim. 'I like the dress you're wearing. You'd look silly wearing a kettle.'

Davy thought that was funny—but he liked the one about the hot cross bunnies better.

'You haven't changed, I see,' said Grandma West glumly as she filled the kettle with water. 'You won't gain anything by all that silliness.'

'Laughter is the best medicine, Mother,' Uncle Jim said.

Grandma sniffed. 'Laughter won't cure my aching old bones, will it?'

Davy felt sorry about Grandma's aching old bones. And when Uncle Jim went out again after lunch, he didn't ask if he could go too. He had a plan that just might make Grandma feel better... All he needed was some card, and his felt-tips.

'Have you ever been to a pantomime?' Uncle Jim asked Davy as soon as he got back. In his hand were some tickets. 'I've reserved some seats for *Jack and the Beanstalk*,' he said. 'We're going tonight.'

'Great!' shouted Davy, jumping up and down. 'The pantomime—brilliant!'

'I got an extra ticket,' Uncle Jim told him. 'Do you think your friend next door would like to come with us?'

Davy stared at him. Invite Oliver to go to the pantomime with them? Oliver would jump at the chance, Davy knew. But he'd much rather have Uncle Jim to himself.

But then, Oliver did need a friend. 'I'll go round and ask him,' he said.

Oliver was pleased, and his mum and dad said he could go with them. But Davy wasn't sure whether he was pleased or not that Oliver was coming.

The seats were good ones, right in the middle, near the front of the theatre. Davy sat between Uncle Jim and Oliver.

The pantomime was great. Jack's mother was acted by a man dressed in lady's clothes and wearing silly yellow-and-red-striped stockings, and Jack was played by a girl with very long legs, dressed as a boy. And Jack's cow was two men wearing a cow's costume. When Jack's mother said she was going to milk the cow, it did a little dance, tripped over its own feet and fell down with a thud. One of the men inside the cow handed out a bottle of milk to her, and everybody laughed.

But best of all was Gonzo, the funny man. Davy and Oliver and Uncle Jim rocked with laughter at some of the jokes he told. He told one about a gardener who went over his potato patch with a heavy roller because he wanted to grow mashed potatoes.

Then he said, 'What do you get when you pour hot water down a rabbit hole?'

And before he could stop himself, Davy shouted out, 'Hot cross bunnies!'

Everybody laughed, and Oliver hooted and dug him in the ribs. But Gonzo looked across the audience towards them. 'Who stole my line?' he said sternly.

'Me.' Davy stood up, his heart thumping. Was Gonzo angry with him?

Gonzo beckoned with his hand. 'You want to be a funny man? Well, come on up here and let's see what you can do!'

A smiling lady showed him the way to the steps to go up on to the stage. Davy looked around him. The lights were very bright, but he could just see what looked like a sea of faces below him. He swallowed.

Gonzo asked his name. 'Right, Davy,' he said. 'Know any more jokes?' Davy nodded. 'OK, let's hear them.'

Davy thought for a minute, took a deep breath, and started.

He told every one of the jokes he had learnt that morning from Uncle Jim, as well as a few more of his own, and the audience laughed just as loudly as they had when Gonzo told jokes. At last, he couldn't think of any more.

'Is that it, then?' asked Gonzo.

'I think so.'

Gonzo beckoned to a man standing at the side of the stage, and the man walked over and handed Davy a carrier-bag. 'These are your wages for being a terrific funny man,' Gonzo said. Then he pretended to hit Davy over the head. 'And that's for stealing my line!'

'You were great!' Oliver told him when he got back to his seat.

Davy looked into the bag. It was full of sweets and chocolates and bags of crisps. And in a big square box was a shiny yellow car.

'Have some lemon drops,' he said, offering the bag to Oliver. Oliver took out a packet of fruit gums and shared them with Davy.

Perhaps Oliver wasn't too bad after all, Davy thought.

The next day, instead of Grandma West coming to their house, they went to hers—and Oliver went with them. In spite of her aching bones she had made a big bowl of crunchy salad and a pile of ham sandwiches. And there was a creamy pink-and-white trifle too. While they ate, Davy told her all about the pantomime.

'Uncle Jim got some preserved seats,' he said, and wondered why Uncle Jim laughed.

'You mean reserved seats,' he told Davy.

After tea, Mum and Dad did the washing up so that Grandma could rest. She sat down very carefully, holding her aching back. Suddenly, Davy remembered the surprise he had made for her yesterday. He went and got it out of his coat pocket.

'It's a get-well card, Grandma,' he told her, rubbing it to get rid of the creases. 'I made it all by myself.'

Grandma looked at the card. On the front it said, 'May your akeing bones get well soon'.

'The spelling might not be quite right,' Davy told her.

She opened the card. Inside was Davy's picture—a horse galloping around a field of poppies. He had spent a long time colouring in each red poppy very carefully.

Without warning, Grandma West's shoulders started to shake. What was wrong with her? Were her aching bones worse? Davy bent over her and she looked up at him.

She was laughing.

Davy stared. She was laughing as he had never seen her laugh, holding herself around her middle and rocking to and fro. She was laughing at his card! She passed the card to Uncle Jim, and he started to laugh too.

'What a marvellous idea to cheer me up, Davy,'

she said shakily, wiping her eyes. 'I haven't had such a good laugh for a long, long time.'

'I told you that laughter was the best medicine,' said Uncle Jim. He slapped Davy's shoulder. 'The horse is fantastic, Davy—it reminds me of the pantomime cow.'

Davy, trying not to be hurt because they were laughing at his drawing, took the card back and looked again at his horse.

It was true. The horse *was* like the pantomime cow—its front knees and its back knees both bent forward, like people's knees did. He'd forgotten that horses' back legs went the other way. Davy chuckled. He leant across and showed the picture to Oliver, pointing to the horse's funny knees. He started to laugh, and Oliver laughed too. They all laughed together, making so much noise that Mum and Dad came in from the kitchen to see what all the noise was about.

'That's done me the world of good,' said Grandma West at last. 'Thank you, Davy. I feel wonderful!'

Davy went back to his coat pocket and brought out a big bag of jelly babies. 'These are for you,' he said, putting the bag on Grandma's knee. 'They were part of my wages for being a funny man at the pantomime last night.'

'He was brilliant,' Oliver told her. 'He went up on the stage and told all Uncle Jim's jokes!'

Grandma West took a jelly baby and settled back in her armchair. 'Is that so?' she said with a chuckle. 'And to think I said that you'd never gain anything from silliness!'

It was just after breakfast on Christmas Day. Davy rode up and down the street on his brand new stunt bike.

'Look—I can do wheelies on it!' he shouted to Oliver. 'Go and get yours, then we can both do stunts.'

Oliver shook his head doubtfully, and Davy thought that Oliver must have had Christmas presents that he would want to play with too.

'Well, we could play later if you want to go in now,' Davy said.

But to his surprise, Oliver shook his head again.

Davy wheeled round and round on his bike and came to a stop in front of Oliver. 'What shall we do then?'

'We could go to your house and play with some of your presents,' Oliver suggested, and Davy grinned at him.

He knew that Oliver liked coming round to his house, even when Amy grizzled or Grandma West was in a grumbly mood.

'We could play "Hungry Hippos", ' he told Oliver. 'But later on we're all going out. It's the Christmas morning service at church.'

He waited for Oliver to turn up his nose and say, 'Boring!'

But he didn't. Oliver picked up Davy's bike and headed up the driveway of his house.

'Great,' he said. 'Do you think your mum and dad will let me come, too?'

'No problem!' said Davy. 'Come on.'

Also from Lion Publishing

THE BOY WHO WOULDN'T
Veronica Heley

'I'll be so bad to the new people that they'll sell their house back to the Biker. Then everything will be all right again,' thought Joe.

It is the worst day of Joe's life. His only friend has moved away and there are new people living next door. But not for long—if Joe has anything to do with it.

ISBN 0 7459 1967 7

Other stories from LION PUBLISHING for you to enjoy: